Oh, Daddy!

Bob Shea

Balzer + Bray

An Imprint of HarperCollins Publishers

Balzer & Bray is an imprint of HarperCollins Publishers.

Oh, Daddy!
Copyright © 2010 by Bob Shea

For information address
HarperCollins Children's Books,
a division of HarperCollins Publishers,
10 East 53rd Street, New York, NY 10022.
www.harpercollinschildrens.com

Library of Congress Cataloging-in-Publication Data
Shea, Bob.
    Oh, Daddy! / Bob Shea. — 1st ed.
       p.   cm.
    Summary: A young hippopotamus shows his father the right
way to do things, such as getting dressed, watering the flowers,
and especially giving big hugs.
    ISBN 978-0-06-173080-1
    [1. Fathers and sons—Fiction.   2. Hippopotamus—Fiction.]
I. Title.
PZ7.S53743Oh 2010   2009020525
[E]—dc22   CIP
                                               AC

Typography by Perfectly Nice
10 11 12 13 14   LEO   10 9 8 7 6 5 4 3 2 1
❖
First Edition

To my dad

I may be little, but I'm as smart as
two eight-year-olds! I'm so smart,
I even show my dad how to do things—
and he's a grown-up!

In the morning, when I'm busy
getting dressed, he asks . . .

"Is **this** how you get dressed?"

"Oh, Daddy!"

"**This** is how you get dressed!"

Then, when we're late to Grandma's, he asks . . .

"**This** is how you get in the car."

See? Easy peasy, mac and cheesy!

"Come on, Daddy!"

Even when I'm eating lunch
I have to stop and help my dad.

"Is **this** how you eat carrots?"

"Oh, Daddy!"

"**This** is how you eat carrots!"

Sometimes I tease Daddy.
Like when he was watering the flowers . . .

"Is **this** how you water the flowers?" he asks.

And no matter how many times I show him,
he always needs help with big hugs!

"Is **this** how you give big hugs?"

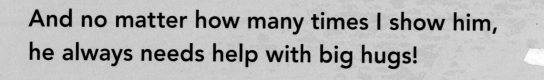

"Oh, Daddy!"

"**This** is how you give big hugs!"

I don't know what my daddy
would do without me.